ME AND MY SISTER

A book to share from

Scallywag Press

FOR MY FAMILY

First published in Great Britain in 2019 by Scallywag Press Ltd,
10 Sutherland Row, London SW1V 4JT.

Art Direction and design by Sarah Finan

Colour separated by Aylesbury Studios, Bromley, Kent, UK

Printed in Malaysia by Tien Wah Press

001

British Library Cataloguing in Publication Data available.

ISBN 978-1-912650-00-2

ME AND MY SISTER

ROSE ROBBINS

Scallywag Press Ltd

LONDON

SHE DOESN'T USE WORDS
BUT SHE SAYS A LOT!

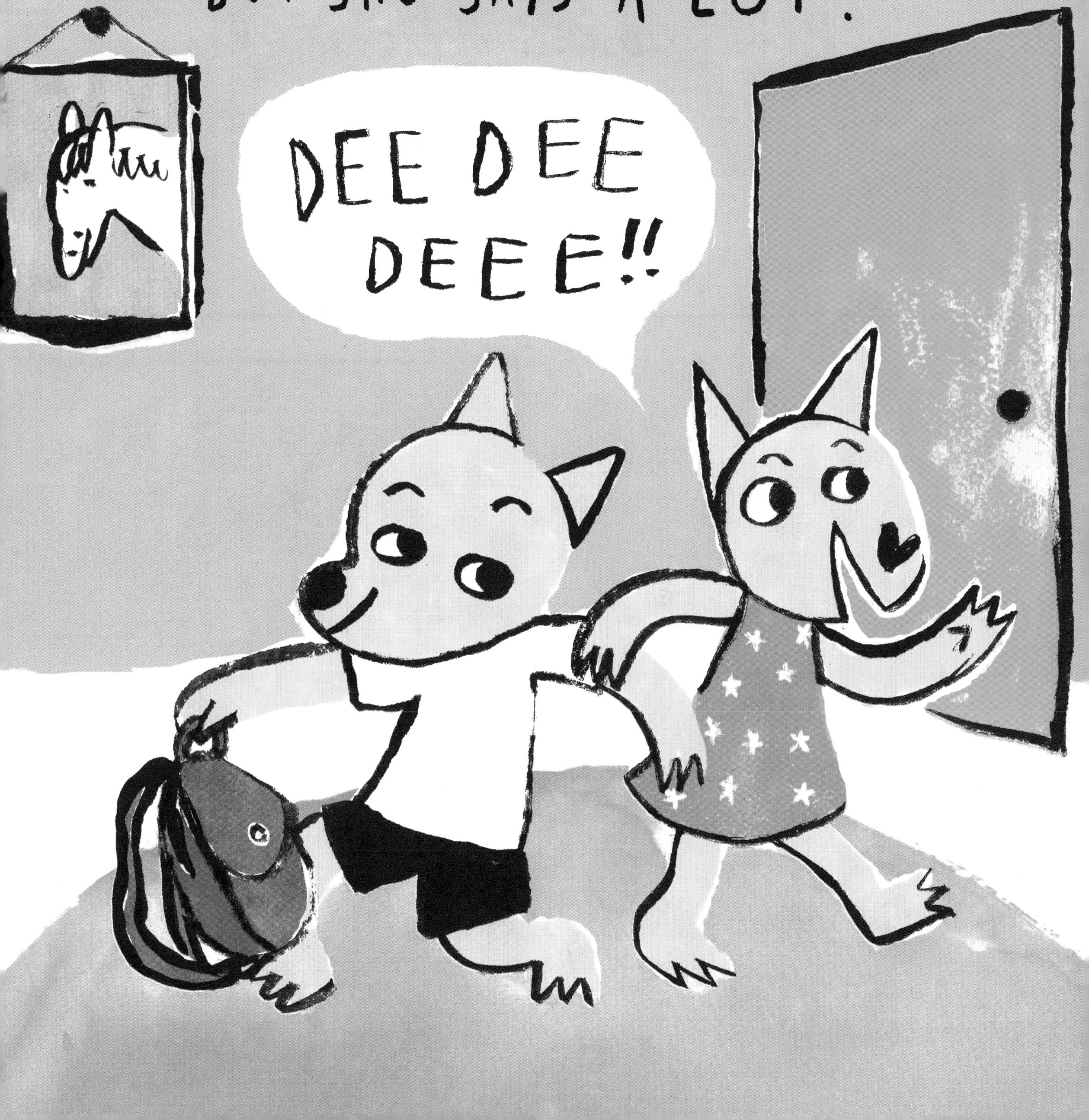

...BUT WE FINISH
AT THE SAME TIME.

MY SISTER LIKES TO WATCH TV BY HERSELF

BUT IT'S **BEST** WHEN WE LISTEN TOGETHER!

SOMETIMES MY SISTER IS RUDE TO NANNA

BUT NANNA UNDERSTANDS

EVEN IF
I DON'T.

SOMETIMES MY SISTER JUST NEEDS TO BE ALONE.

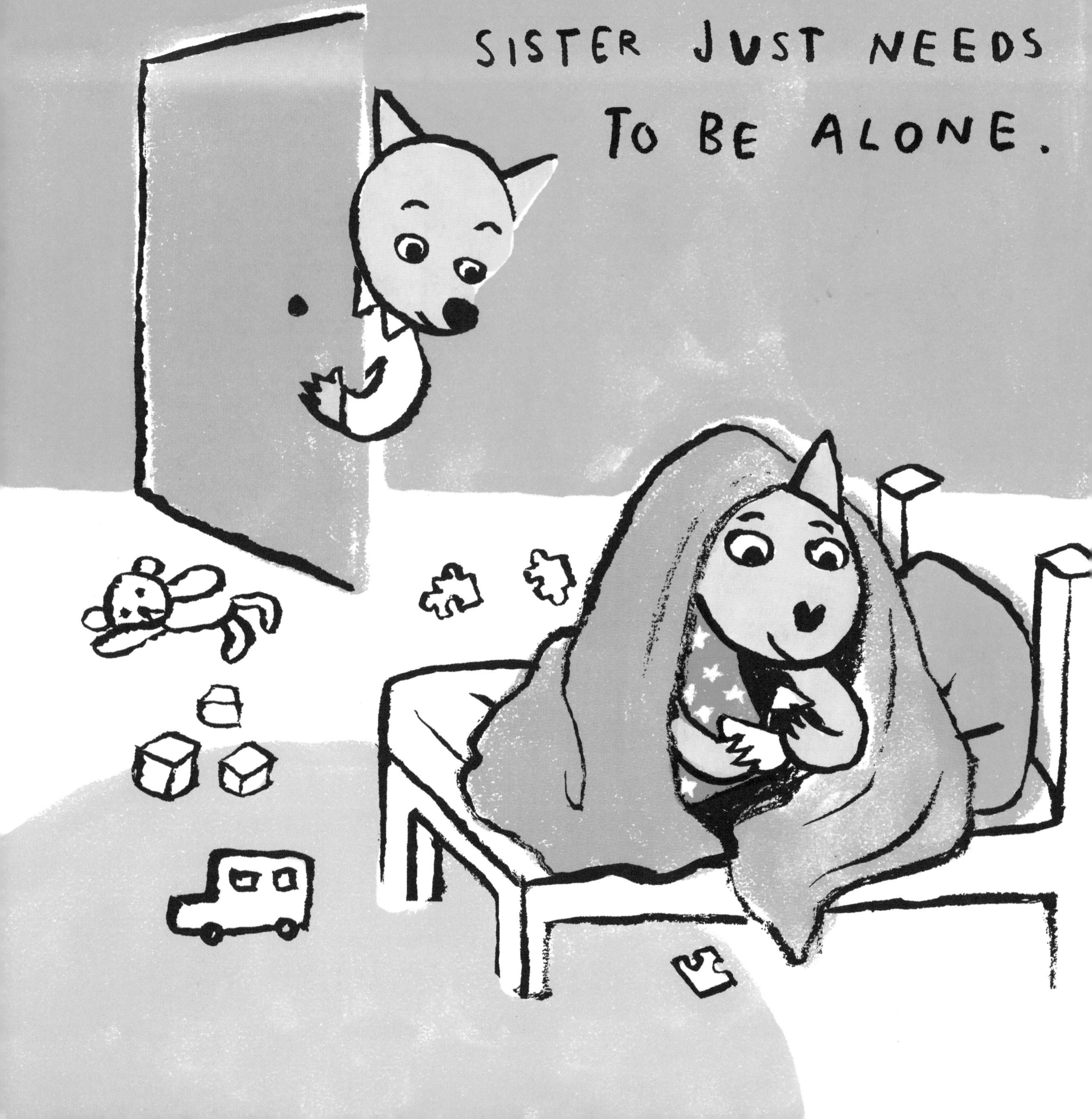

AND SOMETIMES SHE DOESN'T!

ME AND MY SISTER
GO TO DIFFERENT SCHOOLS.

WE DO DIFFERENT THINGS...

...AND WE BOTH LEARN A LOT!

AND MY SISTER DOESN'T.

BUT, IF MY SISTER IS UPSET...

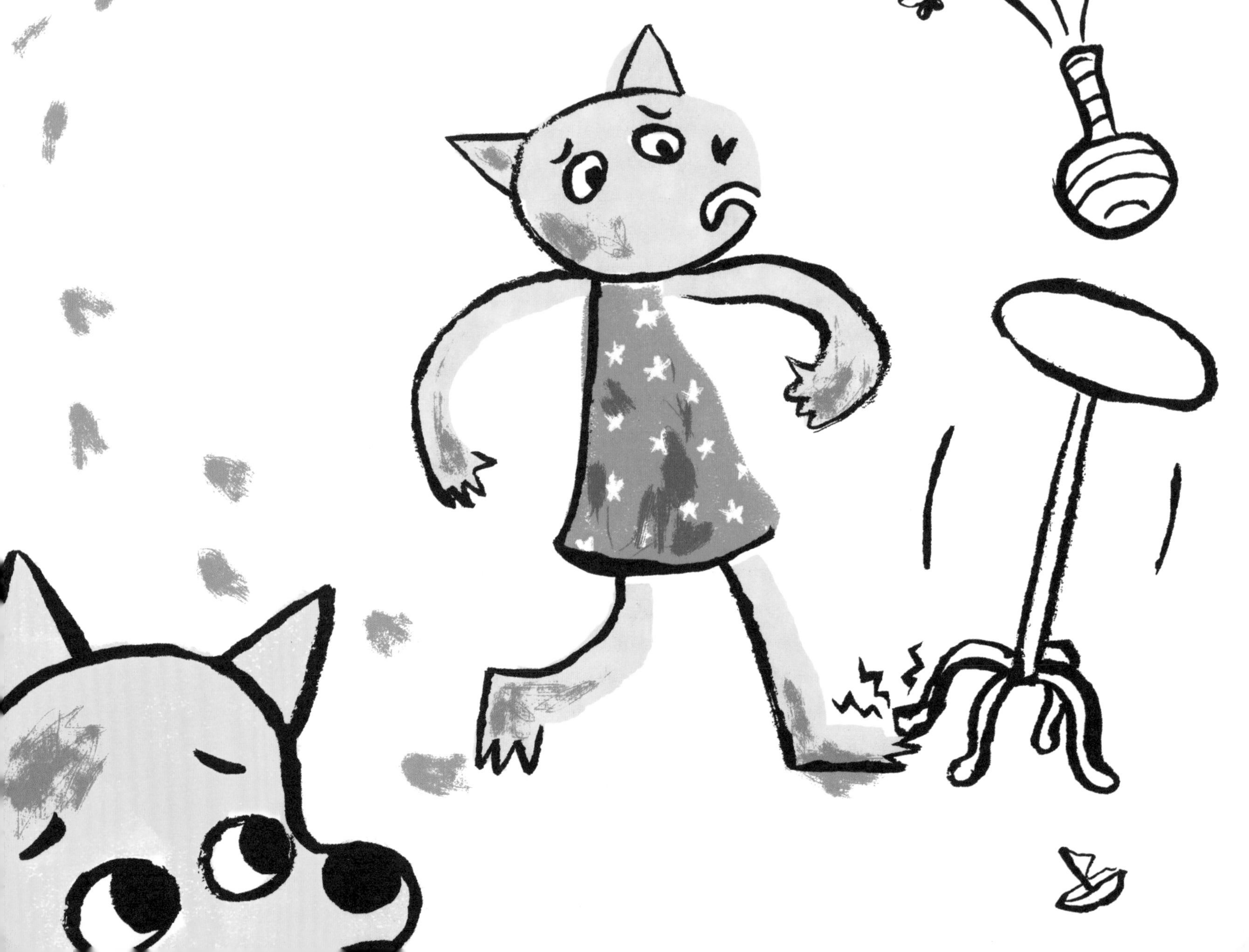

MY SISTER
DOESN'T ALWAYS
LIKE HUGS

SO WE HIGH-FIVE INSTEAD!

ME AND MY SISTER

ARE VERY DIFFERENT...

BUT WE
LOVE EACH OTHER
JUST THE SAME.